Freddy's Fishbowl

Marco White

NEIGHBORHOOD READERS

Rosen Classroom Books & Materials™

New York

Freddy the fish wants a friend.

"Hi, cat. Will you be my friend?"
"No," said the cat.

"Hi, dog. Will you be my friend?"
"No," said the dog.

"Hi, turtle. Will you be my friend?"
"No," said the turtle.

"Hi, rabbit. Will you be my friend?"
"No," said the rabbit.

"Hi, fish. Will you be my friend?"
"Yes, I will be your friend!"
said the fish.

"I have a friend!" said Freddy.
"I like my new friend!"